Donkey Ysabel

Donkey Ysabel

By Dorothy O. Van Woerkom
Pictures by Normand Chartier

MACMILLAN PUBLISHING CO., INC.
New York

COLLIER MACMILLAN PUBLISHERS
London

Macmillan Publishing Co., Inc.
866 Third Avenue, New York, N. Y. 10022
Collier Macmillan Canada, Ltd.
Printed in the United States of America

10 9 8 7 6 5 4 3 2 1

LIBRARY OF CONGRESS CATALOGING IN PUBLICATION DATA
Van Woerkom, Dorothy.
  Donkey Ysabel.
  (Ready-to-read)
  SUMMARY: Donkey Ysabel is upset when she is replaced
by a car but proves to her farmer owner that she is
still superior to an automobile.
  [1. Donkeys—Fiction] I. Chartier, Normand,
1945–   II. Title.
PZ7.V39Do   [Fic]   78-5140   ISBN 0–02–791280–9

This is for Marissa, Michele,
Maria and Melissa Feliberty

D.O.V.W.

To Sandy, Molly, Alan and Refna

N.C.

It was a fine Sunday morning.

Donkey Ysabel was going to church.

In the cart behind her
were Papa and Mama
and the two children.
Pig Pedro, Goat Carla,
and Rooster Pepi
watched from the fence.

"How lucky Donkey Ysabel is,"
said Rooster.
Pig blew through his nose.
"Good luck comes and
good luck goes," he said.
Goat shook her head
and waggled her ears.
"What a terrible thing to say!"
"Well, it is true," Pig said.
"Sooner or later
something will go wrong.
It always does."

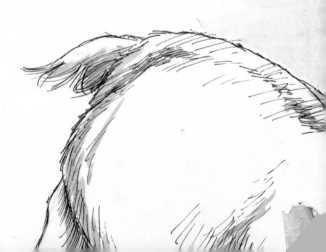

Donkey Ysabel brought her cart
to the church door and nodded
to all the other donkeys.
She was very proud of
her cart and her family.
The people all went
inside the church.
The donkeys waited outside,
talking to each other.
This was the best part
of Sunday!

When the family came out again,
Donkey Ysabel took them home.
Tomorrow she would help Papa
dig up potatoes in the field.
On market day she would take
the potatoes to market.

But when tomorrow came,
Papa was not there.
Mama went to the field
with Donkey Ysabel.
"Where is Papa?"
the animals wondered.
On the next day,
Rooster crowed,
"Papa is home! He has
   brought a new cart
   for Donkey Ysabel!"
Donkey Ysabel ran
with Goat and Pig
to see the new cart.
"That is a strange cart,"
Goat said.

Donkey Ysabel walked all around it.
"It is larger than my old one," she said.
"But I can pull it, I think."

Papa came out of the house
and climbed into the cart.
Mama and the children
climbed in after him.
"Look," said Donkey Ysabel.
"They are ready to go
for an afternoon ride—
but they forgot to
hitch me to my new cart."

She stood in front of the cart
and waited for someone
to hitch her up to it.
Suddenly the cart began to growl.
Gaaa-rrr-uuum! Gaaa-rrr-uuum!
Then it made a great noise.
Aaa-rooo-ooo-ooo-gaaa!

The sound
hurt Donkey Ysabel's ears.
Papa began shouting
and waving
for her to get out of the way.
Donkey Ysabel got out of the way.

16

She watched her new cart
going down the road by itself.
"That is not a cart," she said.
"It can go all by itself.
It must be a strange kind
of *donkey*!"
She began to bray loudly.
"Oh, a new donkey," Goat said.
"What a shame!"
"I told you that something
would go wrong," Pig said.
"A donkey that looks like a cart
is *very* wrong," said Rooster.

The next day Donkey Ysabel
took her cart to the field
to help Papa.
"That new donkey is lazy," she said.
"It did not come to help Papa."
"It does not even speak
when I talk to it," Rooster said.
"Maybe its feet hurt," Goat said.
"Have you looked at those feet?"
"That new donkey lets you
do all the work," Pig said.
"I call that very bad luck,
Donkey Ysabel."

On market day

Donkey Ysabel waited for Papa

near the barn door.

When Papa came,

the children came with him.

So did the new donkey.

Donkey Ysabel stamped her foot.

"I will not let that donkey

take my cart to market!"

But Papa did not bring

Donkey Ysabel's cart.

He and the children tied
the sacks of potatoes
all over the new donkey.
Inside, outside, and topside
they tied the sacks.
"What are they doing?" Rooster asked.
"They never tied sacks
onto Donkey Ysabel."

21

"That is because I do not look like
a *cart*!" Donkey Ysabel said.
Papa climbed inside
the new donkey.
It began to growl again.
Gaaa-rrr-uuum! Gaaa-rrr-uuum!
Mama came out of the house
and climbed in beside Papa.
Aaa-rooo-ooo-ooo-gaaa!
said the donkey
that looked like a cart.
The children jumped in the back,
and the donkey ran down the road.
"That is a funny way
to ride on a donkey," Goat said.
"No good can come of it," said Pig.

23

Donkey Ysabel sat down
in the middle of the road.
"When that new donkey comes home
I will make it run away."
But when the new donkey
came home, something
was wrong with it.
It moved very slowly.
It was spitting up hot water
and spilling it all down its front.

"Look at that," Donkey Ysabel said.
"It is hot and tired.
   A little trip to market—
   which I can make easily—
   is too much for this lazy donkey."

Mama and Papa and the children
jumped out of the donkey.
Papa opened the donkey's mouth
and looked inside.
Now the donkey was smoking!
Mama ran for some water.
Papa poured the water
into the donkey's mouth.
The smoke went away
and the donkey
stopped spitting.
Donkey Ysabel walked up behind it.
She kicked hard at one of its feet.
Sssssst! said the foot.
And the foot kept on saying
Sssssst!

It got smaller
and smaller
and smaller.

The donkey began to tip
just a little.
"There!" said Donkey Ysabel.
"I have broken its foot."
And she brayed a loud,
laughing bray.
The new donkey said nothing.

28

Rooster crowed and
hopped around on one foot.
Goat danced and bleated.
Papa ran around,
shouting and shaking his fist
at Donkey Ysabel.

"You should not have done that,"
Pig said. "I think you have
made things much worse."
Mama shooed Donkey Ysabel
back to the field.
Papa knelt down by the sick donkey
to look at its foot.

"Why are they mad at *me*?"
Donkey Ysabel wondered.
"I never spit and smoke.
I hurry to bring Papa
home from the market."

That night
Papa put the new donkey
in Donkey Ysabel's shed,
even though its foot
was well again.
Donkey Ysabel
had to sleep in the barn
with the cart and the plow
and all the old potato sacks.
Pig shook his head sadly.
"Ever since that donkey came,
nothing has gone right
for Donkey Ysabel!"

On Sunday the new donkey
took the family to church.
"After you worked so hard,"
Goat said. "What a shame!"
"Maybe you will never see
your friends again,"
Rooster said.
"My friends will laugh
to see that donkey in my place,"
said Donkey Ysabel.
She began to cry.
"Never mind," Pig said.
"Sooner or later
everything will come right again.
It always does."

"Look!" cried Rooster,
 pointing down the road.
 Mama, Papa, and the children
 were all walking home!
 They hurried up to Donkey Ysabel,
 petting her and laughing.
 Papa brought the cart and
 hitched her to it.
"I must be going to church!"
 Donkey Ysabel said.
"But where is that new donkey?"

She trotted off,
pulling the family
in the cart.
Donkey Ysabel
turned a corner in the road.
There was the new donkey.
It had broken another foot.
Donkey Ysabel brayed
a great, laughing bray
and trotted by.

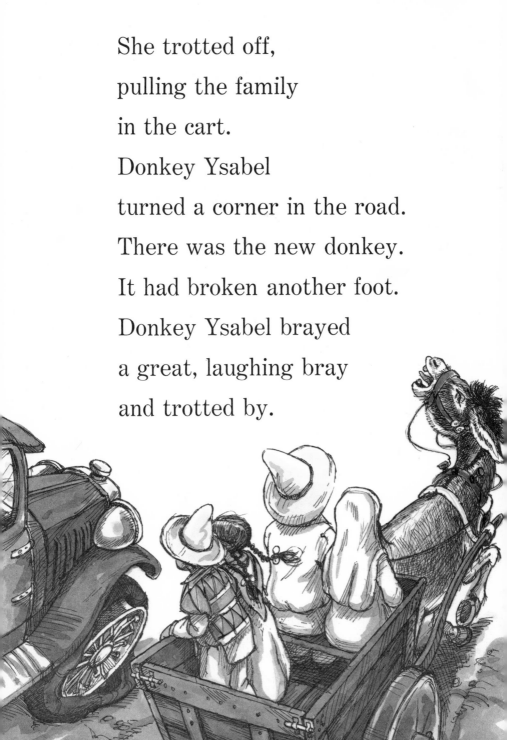

That evening
Donkey Ysabel took Papa
to fix the new donkey's foot.
Papa brought the donkey home,
and Donkey Ysabel followed.
Papa put the new donkey in the barn
with the cart and the plow
and all the old potato sacks.
He put Donkey Ysabel
in her own shed.
She made a lovely bed in the straw
and went to sleep.
The next day
Papa took the new donkey
to dig up potatoes.
They worked all that day,
and the next, and the next.

38

Donkey Ysabel rested
and played with Pig,
Goat, and Rooster.
When market day came,
Papa put the sacks of potatoes
into Donkey Ysabel's cart.
"Look at that!" she said.
"I am going to market!"

On every working day
the other donkey
went to the field with Papa.
If it hurt its foot
or got sick again,
Donkey Ysabel went instead.
Every market day
Donkey Ysabel went to market.
Every Sunday
she went to church.

"That other donkey is good only
for digging potatoes," said Rooster.
"But Papa knows how well
you do *everything*,
Donkey Ysabel," Goat said.
"Papa cannot be late for church
or market, so he does not want
to take that lazy donkey."

Donkey Ysabel
brayed with happiness.
"I have learned something," she said.
"No matter how bad things are,
they always get better."
Pig snorted and puffed himself up.
"That is just what I have been
telling you."

Donkey Ysabel pushed him
into a puddle of mud.
"Tell it to yourself
if Papa ever brings
home a new *pig*!" she said.

44

DOROTHY O. VAN WOERKOM was born and grew up in Buffalo, New York. As a young writer, she won a number of awards in statewide essay contests. Among her popular books for beginning readers are *Sea Frog, City Frog, Abu Ali, Harry and Shellburt* (an ALA Notable Book) and *The Friends of Abu Ali*. She and her husband live in Houston, Texas.

NORMAND CHARTIER was born and raised in rural northeastern Connecticut. He attended the University of Connecticut, where he fitted in art classes between the football seasons. He now works for an advertising agency and illustrates children's books, *Donkey Ysabel* being the seventh. Normand Chartier lives with his wife and daughter in Brooklyn, Connecticut.

Ready for fun?

Enjoy these Ready-to-Read animal tales.

WISH AGAIN, BIG BEAR
By Richard J. Margolis/Illustrated by Robert Lopshire
Clever Fish bargains with Big Bear for his life. "Readable and entertaining—good fare for even the slowest." —*School Library Journal*

THE KOMODO DRAGON'S JEWELS
Written and illustrated by Diane Redfield Massie
A great, green lizard causes an uproar aboard a cruise ship in "a rollicking tale of mistaken identity." —*School Library Journal*

THE STORY SNAIL
Written and illustrated by Anne Rockwell
"[This] interlocking chain-of-events story about a boy's quest for the silver snail that has taught him 100 stories....possesses an artless simplicity." —*Booklist*

SOPHIE AND GUSSIE
By Marjorie Weinman Sharmat/Illustrated by Lillian Hoban
Four funny episodes in the best friendship of two squirrels. "The illustrations are plentiful, the heroines lovable, and the effect enjoyable." —*Library Journal*

THE TRIP
And Other Sophie and Gussie Stories
By Marjorie Weinman Sharmat/Illustrated by Lillian Hoban
More comical stories about the scatter-brained, charming squirrels first met in *Sophie and Gussie.*

MITCHELL IS MOVING
By Marjorie Weinman Sharmat/Illustrated by Jose Aruego and Ariane Dewey
Mitchell the dinosaur finds that a new home is not all good if his neighbor Margo isn't there in a warm and funny story about friendship.

HARRY AND SHELLBURT
By Dorothy O. Van Woerkom/Illustrated by Erick Ingraham
A.L.A. Notable 1977. A hilarious re-running of the famous race between the tortoise and the hare. "A memorable beginning reader." —*Booklist* (starred review)

DONKEY YSABEL
By Dorothy O. Van Woerkom/Illustrated by Normand Chartier
Donkey Ysabel's pride is hurt when Papa brings home a car—but she manages to get the best of the "new donkey."

LITTLE NEW KANGAROO
By Bernard Wiseman/Illustrated by Robert Lopshire
With Mother Kangaroo lending a helpful pouch, a young kangaroo picks up four friends on his first jaunt into the Australian countryside.